The Gold-Bug

by Edgar Allan Poe

What ho! what ho! this fellow is dancing mad!

He hath been bitten by the Tarantula.

—All in the Wrong.

Many years ago, I contracted an intimacy with a Mr. William Legrand. He was of an ancient Huguenot family, and had once been wealthy: but a series of misfortunes had reduced him to want. To avoid the mortification consequent upon his disasters, he left New Orleans, the city of his forefathers, and took up his residence at Sullivan's Island, near Charleston, South Carolina.

This island is a very singular one. It consists of little else than the sea sand, and is about three miles long. Its breadth at no point exceeds a quarter of a mile. It is separated from the mainland by a scarcely perceptible creek, oozing its way through a wilderness of reeds and slime, a favorite resort of the marsh hen. The vegetation, as might be supposed, is scant, or at least dwarfish. No trees of any magnitude are to be seen. Near the western extremity, where Fort Moultrie stands, and where are some miserable frame buildings, tenanted, during summer, by the fugitives from Charleston dust and fever, may be found, indeed, the bristly palmetto; but the whole island, with the exception of this western point, and a line of hard, white beach on the seacoast, is covered with a dense undergrowth of the sweet myrtle so much prized by the horticulturists of England. The shrub here often attains the height of fifteen or twenty feet, and forms an almost impenetrable coppice, burdening the air with its fragrance.

In the inmost recesses of this coppice, not far from the eastern or more remote end of the island, Legrand had built himself a small hut, which he occupied when I first, by mere accident, made his acquaintance. This soon ripened into friendship—for there was much in the recluse to excite interest and esteem. I found him well educated, with unusual powers of mind, but infected with misanthropy, and subject to perverse moods of alternate enthusiasm and melancholy. He had with him many books, but rarely employed them. His chief amusements were gunning and fishing, or sauntering along the beach and through the myrtles, in quest of shells or entomological specimens—his collection of the latter might have been envied by a Swammerdamm. In these excursions he was usually accompanied by an old negro, called Jupiter, who had been manumitted before the reverses of the family, but who could be induced, neither by threats nor by promises, to abandon what he considered his right of attendance upon the footsteps of his young "Massa Will." It is not improbable that the relatives of Legrand, conceiving him to be somewhat unsettled in intellect, had contrived to instill this obstinacy into Jupiter, with a view to the supervision and guardianship of the wanderer.

The winters in the latitude of Sullivan's Island are seldom very severe, and in the fall of the year it is a rare event indeed when a fire is considered necessary. About the middle of October, 18—, there occurred, however, a day of remarkable chilliness. Just before sunset I scrambled my way through the evergreens to the hut of my friend, whom I had not visited for several weeks—my residence being, at that time, in Charleston, a distance of nine miles from the island, while the facilities of passage and repassage were very far behind those of the present day. Upon reaching the hut I rapped, as was my custom, and getting no reply, sought for the key where I knew it was secreted, unlocked the door, and went in. A fine fire was blazing upon the hearth. It was a novelty, and by no means an ungrateful one. I threw off an overcoat, took an armchair by the crackling logs, and awaited patiently the arrival of my hosts.

Soon after dark they arrived, and gave me a most cordial welcome. Jupiter, grinning from ear to ear, bustled about to prepare some marsh hens for supper. Legrand was in one of his fits—how else shall I term them?—of enthusiasm. He had found an unknown bivalve, forming a new genus, and, more than this, he had hunted down and secured, with Jupiter's assistance, a scarabaeus which he believed to be totally new, but in respect to which he wished to have my opinion on the morrow.

"And why not to-night?" I asked, rubbing my hands over the blaze, and wishing the whole tribe of scarabaei at the devil.

"Ah, if I had only known you were here!" said Legrand, "but it's so long since I saw you; and how could I foresee that you would pay me a visit this very night of all others? As I was coming home I met Lieutenant G——, from the fort, and, very foolishly, I lent him the bug; so it will be impossible for you to see it until the morning. Stay here to-night, and I will send Jup down for it at sunrise. It is the loveliest thing in creation!"

"What?—sunrise?"

"Nonsense! no!—the bug. It is of a brilliant gold color—about the size of a large hickory nut—with two jet black spots near one extremity of the back, and another, somewhat longer, at the other. The antennae are—"

"Dey ain't NO tin in him, Massa Will, I keep a tellin' on you," here interrupted Jupiter; "de bug is a goole-bug, solid, ebery bit of him, inside and all, sep him wing—neber feel half so hebby a bug in my life."

"Well, suppose it is, Jup," replied Legrand, somewhat more earnestly, it seemed to me, than the case demanded; "is that any reason for your letting the birds burn? The color"—here he turned to me—"is really almost enough to warrant Jupiter's idea. You never saw a more brilliant metallic luster than the scales emit— but of this you cannot judge till to-morrow. In the meantime I can give you some idea of the shape." Saying this, he seated himself at a small table, on which were a pen and ink, but no paper. He looked for some in a drawer, but found none.

"Never mind," he said at length, "this will answer;" and he drew from his waistcoat pocket a scrap of what I took to be very dirty foolscap, and made upon it a rough drawing with the pen. While he did this, I retained my seat by the fire, for I was still chilly. When the design was complete, he handed it to me without rising. As I received it, a loud growl was heard, succeeded by a scratching at the door. Jupiter opened it, and a large Newfoundland, belonging to Legrand, rushed in, leaped upon my shoulders, and loaded me with caresses; for I had shown him much attention during previous visits. When his gambols were over, I looked at the paper, and, to speak the truth, found myself not a little puzzled at what my friend had depicted.

"Well!" I said, after contemplating it for some minutes, "this IS a strange scarabaeus, I must confess; new to me; never saw anything like it before—unless it was a skull, or a death's head, which it more nearly resembles than anything else that has come under MY observation."

"A death's head!" echoed Legrand. "Oh—yes—well, it has something of that appearance upon paper, no doubt. The two upper black spots look like eyes, eh? and the longer one at the bottom like a mouth— and then the shape of the whole is oval."

"Perhaps so," said I; "but, Legrand, I fear you are no artist. I must wait until I see the beetle itself, if I am to form any idea of its personal appearance."

"Well, I don't know," said he, a little nettled, "I draw tolerably— SHOULD do it at least—have had good masters, and flatter myself that I am not quite a blockhead."

"But, my dear fellow, you are joking then," said I, "this is a very passable SKULL—indeed, I may say that it is a very EXCELLENT skull, according to the vulgar notions about such specimens of physiology—and your scarabaeus must be the queerest scarabaeus in the world if it resembles it. Why, we may get up a very thrilling bit of superstition upon this hint. I presume you will call the bug Scarabaeus caput hominis, or something of that kind—there are many similar titles in the Natural Histories. But where are the antennae you spoke of?"

"The antennae!" said Legrand, who seemed to be getting unaccountably warm upon the subject; "I am sure you must see the antennae. I made them as distinct as they are in the original insect, and I presume that is sufficient."

"Well, well," I said, "perhaps you have—still I don't see them;" and I handed him the paper without additional remark, not wishing to ruffle his temper; but I was much surprised at the turn affairs had taken; his ill humor puzzled me—and, as for the drawing of the beetle, there were positively NO antennae visible, and the whole DID bear a very close resemblance to the ordinary cuts of a death's head.

He received the paper very peevishly, and was about to crumple it, apparently to throw it in the fire, when a casual glance at the design seemed suddenly to rivet his attention. In an instant his face grew violently red—in another excessively pale. For some minutes he continued to scrutinize the drawing minutely where he sat. At length he arose, took a candle from the table, and proceeded to seat himself upon a sea chest in the farthest corner of the room. Here again he made an anxious examination of the paper, turning it in all directions. He said nothing, however, and his conduct greatly astonished me; yet I thought it prudent not to exacerbate the growing moodiness of his temper by any comment. Presently he took from his coat pocket a wallet, placed the paper carefully in it, and deposited both in a writing desk, which he locked. He now grew more composed in his demeanor; but his original air of enthusiasm had quite disappeared. Yet he seemed not so much sulky as abstracted. As the evening wore away he became more and more absorbed in reverie, from which no sallies of mine could arouse him. It had been my intention to pass the night at the hut, as I had frequently done before, but, seeing my host in this mood, I deemed it proper to take leave. He did not press me to remain, but, as I departed, he shook my hand with even more than his usual cordiality.

It was about a month after this and during the interval I had seen nothing of Legrand when I received a visit, at Charleston, from his man, Jupiter. I had never seen the good old negro look so dispirited, and I feared that some serious disaster had befallen my friend.

"Well, Jup," said I, "what is the matter now?—how is your master?"

"Why, to speak the troof, massa, him not so berry well as mought be."

"Not well! I am truly sorry to hear it. What does he complain of?"

"Dar! dot's it!—him neber 'plain of notin'—but him berry sick for all dat."

"VERY sick, Jupiter!—why didn't you say so at once? Is he confined to bed?"

"No, dat he aint!—he aint 'fin'd nowhar—dat's just whar de shoe pinch—my mind is got to be berry hebby 'bout poor Massa Will."

"Jupiter, I should like to understand what it is you are talking about. You say your master is sick. Hasn't he told you what ails him?"

"Why, massa, 'taint worf while for to git mad about de matter— Massa Will say noffin at all aint de matter wid him—but den what make him go about looking dis here way, wid he head down and he soldiers up, and as white as a goose? And den he keep a syphon all de time—"

"Keeps a what, Jupiter?"

"Keeps a syphon wid de figgurs on de slate—de queerest figgurs I ebber did see. Ise gittin' to be skeered, I tell you. Hab for to keep mighty tight eye 'pon him 'noovers. Todder day he gib me slip 'fore de sun up and was gone de whole ob de blessed day. I had a big stick ready cut for to gib him deuced good beating when he did come—but Ise sich a fool dat I hadn't de heart arter all—he looked so berry poorly."

"Eh?—what?—ah yes!—upon the whole I think you had better not be too severe with the poor fellow—don't flog him, Jupiter—he can't very well stand it—but can you form no idea of what has occasioned this illness, or rather this change of conduct? Has anything unpleasant happened since I saw you?"

"No, massa, dey aint bin noffin onpleasant SINCE den—'twas 'FORE den I'm feared—'twas de berry day you was dare."

"How? what do you mean."

"Why, massa, I mean de bug—dare now."

"The what?"

"De bug—I'm berry sartin dat Massa Will bin bit somewhere 'bout de head by dat goole-bug."

"And what cause have you, Jupiter, for such a supposition?"

"Claws enuff, massa, and mouff, too. I nebber did see sich a deuced bug—he kick and he bite eberyting what cum near him. Massa Will cotch him fuss, but had for to let him go 'gin mighty quick, I tell you—den was de time he must ha' got de bite. I didn't like de look ob de bug mouff, myself, nohow, so I wouldn't take hold oh him wid my finger, but I cotch him wid a piece oh paper dat I found. I rap him up in de paper and stuff a piece of it in he mouff—dat was de way."

"And you think, then, that your master was really bitten by the beetle, and that the bite made him sick?"

"I don't think noffin about it—I nose it. What make him dream 'bout de goole so much, if 'taint cause he bit by the goole-bug? Ise heered 'bout dem goole-bugs 'fore dis."

"But how do you know he dreams about gold?"

"How I know? why, 'cause he talk about it in he sleep—dat's how I nose."

"Well, Jup, perhaps you are right; but to what fortunate circumstance am I to attribute the honor of a visit from you to- day?"

"What de matter, massa?"

"Did you bring any message from Mr. Legrand?"

"No, massa, I bring dis here pissel;" and here Jupiter handed me a note which ran thus:

"MY DEAR ——

"Why have I not seen you for so long a time? I hope you have not been so foolish as to take offense at any little brusquerie of mine; but no, that is improbable.

"Since I saw you I have had great cause for anxiety. I have something to tell you, yet scarcely know how to tell it, or whether I should tell it at all.

"I have not been quite well for some days past, and poor old Jup annoys me, almost beyond endurance, by his well-meant attentions. Would you believe it?—he had prepared a huge stick, the other day, with which to chastise me for giving him the slip, and spending the day, solus, among the hills on the mainland. I verily believe that my ill looks alone saved me a flogging.

"I have made no addition to my cabinet since we met. "If you can, in any way, make it convenient, come over with Jupiter. DO come. I wish to see you

TO-NIGHT, upon business of importance. I assure you that it is of the HIGHEST importance.

"Ever yours,

"WILLIAM LEGRAND."

There was something in the tone of this note which gave me great uneasiness. Its whole style differed materially from that of Legrand. What could he be dreaming of? What new crotchet possessed his excitable brain? What "business of the highest importance" could HE possibly have to transact? Jupiter's account of him boded no good. I dreaded lest the continued pressure of misfortune had, at length, fairly unsettled the reason of my friend. Without a moment's hesitation, therefore, I prepared to accompany the negro.

Upon reaching the wharf, I noticed a scythe and three spades, all apparently new, lying in the bottom of the boat in which we were to embark.

"What is the meaning of all this, Jup?" I inquired.

"Him syfe, massa, and spade."

"Very true; but what are they doing here?"

"Him de syfe and de spade what Massa Will sis 'pon my buying for him in de town, and de debbil's own lot of money I had to gib for em."

"But what, in the name of all that is mysterious, is your 'Massa Will' going to do with scythes and spades?"

"Dat's more dan I know, and debbil take me if I don't b'lieve 'tis more dan he know too. But it's all cum ob de bug."

Finding that no satisfaction was to be obtained of Jupiter, whose whole intellect seemed to be absorbed by "de bug," I now stepped into the boat, and made sail. With a fair and strong breeze we soon ran into the little cove to the northward of Fort Moultrie, and a walk of some two miles brought us to the hut. It was about three in the afternoon when we arrived. Legrand had been awaiting us in eager expectation. He grasped my hand with a nervous empressement which alarmed me and strengthened the suspicions already entertained. His countenance was pale even to ghastliness, and his deep-set eyes glared with unnatural luster. After some inquiries respecting his health, I asked him, not knowing what better to say, if he had yet obtained the scarabaeus from Lieutenant G——.

"Oh, yes," he replied, coloring violently, "I got it from him the next morning. Nothing should tempt me to part with that scarabaeus. Do you know that Jupiter is quite right about it?"

"In what way?" I asked, with a sad foreboding at heart.

"In supposing it to be a bug of REAL GOLD." He said this with an air of profound seriousness, and I felt inexpressibly shocked.

"This bug is to make my fortune," he continued, with a triumphant smile; "to reinstate me in my family possessions. Is it any wonder, then, that I prize it? Since Fortune has thought fit to bestow it upon me, I have only to use it properly, and I shall arrive at the gold of which it is the index. Jupiter, bring me that scarabaeus!"

"What! de bug, massa? I'd rudder not go fer trubble dat bug; you mus' git him for your own self." Hereupon Legrand arose, with a grave and stately air, and brought me the beetle from a glass case in which it was enclosed. It was a beautiful scarabaeus, and, at that time, unknown to naturalists—of course a great prize in a scientific point of view. There were two round black spots near one extremity of the back, and a long one near the other. The scales were exceedingly hard and glossy, with all the appearance of burnished gold. The weight of the insect was very remarkable, and, taking all things into consideration, I could hardly blame Jupiter for his opinion respecting it; but what to make of Legrand's concordance with that opinion, I could not, for the life of me, tell.

"I sent for you," said he, in a grandiloquent tone, when I had completed my examination of the beetle, "I sent for you that I might have your counsel and assistance in furthering the views of Fate and of the bug—"

"My dear Legrand," I cried, interrupting him, "you are certainly unwell, and had better use some little precautions. You shall go to bed, and I will remain with you a few days, until you get over this. You are feverish and—"

"Feel my pulse," said he.

I felt it, and, to say the truth, found not the slightest indication of fever.

"But you may be ill and yet have no fever. Allow me this once to prescribe for you. In the first place go to bed. In the next—"

"You are mistaken," he interposed, "I am as well as I can expect to be under the excitement which I suffer. If you really wish me well, you will relieve this excitement."

"And how is this to be done?"

"Very easily. Jupiter and myself are going upon an expedition into the hills, upon the mainland, and, in this expedition, we shall need the aid of some person in whom we can confide. You are the only one we can trust.

Whether we succeed or fail, the excitement which you now perceive in me will be equally allayed."

"I am anxious to oblige you in any way," I replied; "but do you mean to say that this infernal beetle has any connection with your expedition into the hills?"

"It has."

"Then, Legrand, I can become a party to no such absurd proceeding."

"I am sorry—very sorry—for we shall have to try it by ourselves."

"Try it by yourselves! The man is surely mad!—but stay!—how long do you propose to be absent?"

"Probably all night. We shall start immediately, and be back, at all events, by sunrise."

"And will you promise me, upon your honor, that when this freak of yours is over, and the bug business good God! settled to your satisfaction, you will then return home and follow my advice implicitly, as that of your physician?"

"Yes; I promise; and now let us be off, for we have no time to lose."

With a heavy heart I accompanied my friend. We started about four o'clock—Legrand, Jupiter, the dog, and myself. Jupiter had with him the scythe and spades—the whole of which he insisted upon carrying—more through fear, it seemed to me, of trusting either of the implements within reach of his master, than from any excess of industry or complaisance. His demeanor was dogged in the extreme, and "dat deuced bug" were the sole words which escaped his lips during the journey. For my own part, I had charge of a couple of dark lanterns, while Legrand contented himself with the scarabaeus, which he carried attached to the end of a bit of whipcord; twirling it to and fro, with the air of a conjurer, as he went. When I observed this last, plain evidence of my friend's aberration of mind, I could scarcely refrain from tears. I thought it best, however, to humor his fancy, at least for the present, or until I could adopt some more energetic measures with a chance of success. In the meantime I endeavored, but all in vain, to sound him in regard to the object of the expedition. Having succeeded in inducing me to accompany him, he seemed unwilling to hold conversation upon any topic of minor importance, and to all my questions vouchsafed no other reply than "we shall see!"

We crossed the creek at the head of the island by means of a skiff, and, ascending the high grounds on the shore of the mainland, proceeded in a northwesterly direction, through a tract of country excessively wild and desolate, where no trace of a human footstep was to be seen. Legrand led the way with decision; pausing only for an instant, here and there, to consult what appeared to be certain landmarks of his own contrivance upon a former occasion.

In this manner we journeyed for about two hours, and the sun was just setting when we entered a region infinitely more dreary than any yet seen. It was a species of table-land, near the summit of an almost inaccessible hill, densely wooded from base to pinnacle, and interspersed with huge crags that appeared to lie loosely upon the soil, and in many cases were prevented from precipitating themselves into the valleys below, merely by the support of the trees against which they reclined. Deep ravines, in various directions, gave an air of still sterner solemnity to the scene.

The natural platform to which we had clambered was thickly overgrown with brambles, through which we soon discovered that it would have been impossible to force our way but for the scythe; and Jupiter, by direction of his master, proceeded to clear for us a path to the foot of an enormously tall tulip tree, which stood, with some eight or ten oaks, upon the level, and far surpassed them all, and all other trees which I had then ever seen, in the beauty of its foliage and form, in the wide spread of its branches, and in the general majesty of its appearance. When we reached this tree, Legrand turned to Jupiter, and asked him if he thought he could climb it. The old man seemed a little staggered by the question, and for some moments made no reply. At length he approached the huge trunk, walked slowly around it, and examined it with minute attention. When he had completed his scrutiny, he merely said:

"Yes, massa, Jup climb any tree he ebber see in he life."

"Then up with you as soon as possible, for it will soon be too dark to see what we are about."

"How far mus' go up, massa?" inquired Jupiter.

"Get up the main trunk first, and then I will tell you which way to go—and here—stop! take this beetle with you."

"De bug, Massa Will!—de goole-bug!" cried the negro, drawing back in dismay—"what for mus' tote de bug way up de tree?—d—n if I do!"

"If you are afraid, Jup, a great big negro like you, to take hold of a harmless little dead beetle, why you can carry it up by this string—but, if you do not take it up with you in some way, I shall be under the necessity of breaking your head with this shovel."

"What de matter now, massa?" said Jup, evidently shamed into compliance; "always want for to raise fuss wid old nigger. Was only funnin anyhow. ME feered de bug! what I keer for de bug?" Here he took cautiously hold of the extreme end of the string, and, maintaining the insect as far from his person as circumstances would permit, prepared to ascend the tree.

In youth, the tulip tree, or Liriodendron tulipiferum, the most magnificent of American foresters, has a trunk peculiarly smooth, and often rises to a great height without lateral branches; but, in its riper age, the bark becomes gnarled and uneven, while many short limbs make their appearance on the stem. Thus the difficulty of ascension, in the present case, lay more in semblance than in reality. Embracing the huge cylinder, as closely as possible, with his arms and knees, seizing with his hands some projections, and resting his naked toes upon others, Jupiter, after one or two narrow escapes from falling, at length wriggled himself into the first great fork, and seemed to consider the whole business as virtually accomplished. The RISK of the achievement was, in fact, now over, although the climber was some sixty or seventy feet from the ground.

"Which way mus' go now, Massa Will?" he asked.

"Keep up the largest branch—the one on this side," said Legrand. The negro obeyed him promptly, and apparently with but little trouble; ascending higher and higher, until no glimpse of his squat figure could be obtained through the dense foliage which enveloped it. Presently his voice was heard in a sort of halloo.

"How much fudder is got to go?"

"How high up are you?" asked Legrand.

"Ebber so fur," replied the negro; "can see de sky fru de top oh de tree."

"Never mind the sky, but attend to what I say. Look down the trunk and count the limbs below you on this side. How many limbs have you passed?"

"One, two, tree, four, fibe—I done pass fibe big limb, massa, 'pon dis side."

"Then go one limb higher."

In a few minutes the voice was heard again, announcing that the seventh limb was attained.

"Now, Jup," cried Legrand, evidently much excited, "I want you to work your way out upon that limb as far as you can. If you see anything strange let me know."

By this time what little doubt I might have entertained of my poor friend's insanity was put finally at rest. I had no alternative but to conclude him stricken with lunacy, and I became seriously anxious about getting him home. While I was pondering upon what was best to be done, Jupiter's voice was again heard.

"Mos feered for to ventur pon dis limb berry far—'tis dead limb putty much all de way."

"Did you say it was a DEAD limb, Jupiter?" cried Legrand in a quavering voice.

"Yes, massa, him dead as de door-nail—done up for sartin—done departed dis here life."

"What in the name of heaven shall I do?" asked Legrand, seemingly in the greatest distress.

"Do!" said I, glad of an opportunity to interpose a word, "why come home and go to bed. Come now!—that's a fine fellow. It's getting late, and, besides, you remember your promise."

"Jupiter," cried he, without heeding me in the least, "do you hear me?"

"Yes, Massa Will, hear you ebber so plain."

"Try the wood well, then, with your knife, and see if you think it VERY rotten."

"Him rotten, massa, sure nuff," replied the negro in a few moments, "but not so berry rotten as mought be. Mought venture out leetle way pon de limb by myself, dat's true."

"By yourself!—what do you mean?"

"Why, I mean de bug. 'Tis BERRY hebby bug. Spose I drop him down fuss, an den de limb won't break wid just de weight of one nigger."

"You infernal scoundrel!" cried Legrand, apparently much relieved, "what do you mean by telling me such nonsense as that? As sure as you drop that beetle I'll break your neck. Look here, Jupiter, do you hear me?"

"Yes, massa, needn't hollo at poor nigger dat style."

"Well! now listen!—if you will venture out on the limb as far as you think safe, and not let go the beetle, I'll make you a present of a silver dollar as soon as you get down."

"I'm gwine, Massa Will—deed I is," replied the negro very promptly—"mos out to the eend now."

"OUT TO THE END!" here fairly screamed Legrand; "do you say you are out to the end of that limb?"

"Soon be to de eend, massa—o-o-o-o-oh! Lor-gol-a-marcy! what IS dis here pon de tree?"

"Well!" cried Legrand, highly delighted, "what is it?"

"Why 'taint noffin but a skull—somebody bin lef him head up de tree, and de crows done gobble ebery bit ob de meat off."

"A skull, you say!—very well,—how is it fastened to the limb?— what holds it on?"

"Sure nuff, massa; mus look. Why dis berry curious sarcumstance, pon my word—dare's a great big nail in de skull, what fastens ob it on to de tree."

"Well now, Jupiter, do exactly as I tell you—do you hear?"

"Yes, massa."

"Pay attention, then—find the left eye of the skull."

"Hum! hoo! dat's good! why dey ain't no eye lef at all."

"Curse your stupidity! do you know your right hand from your left?"

"Yes, I knows dat—knows all about dat—'tis my lef hand what I chops de wood wid."

"To be sure! you are left-handed; and your left eye is on the same side as your left hand. Now, I suppose, you can find the left eye of the skull, or the place where the left eye has been. Have you found it?"

Here was a long pause. At length the negro asked:

"Is de lef eye of de skull pon de same side as de lef hand of de skull too?—cause de skull aint got not a bit oh a hand at all— nebber mind! I got de lef eye now—here de lef eye! what mus do wid it?"

Let the beetle drop through it, as far as the string will reach— but be careful and not let go your hold of the string."

"All dat done, Massa Will; mighty easy ting for to put de bug fru de hole—look out for him dare below!"

During this colloquy no portion of Jupiter's person could be seen; but the beetle, which he had suffered to descend, was now visible at the end of the string, and glistened, like a globe of burnished gold, in the last rays of the setting sun, some of which still faintly illumined the eminence upon which we stood. The scarabaeus hung quite clear of any branches, and, if allowed to fall, would have fallen at our feet. Legrand immediately took the scythe, and cleared with it a circular space, three or four yards in diameter, just beneath the insect, and, having accomplished this, ordered Jupiter to let go the string and come down from the tree.

Driving a peg, with great nicety, into the ground, at the precise spot where the beetle fell, my friend now produced from his pocket a tape measure. Fastening one end of this at that point of the trunk of the tree which was nearest the peg, he unrolled it till it reached the peg and thence further unrolled it, in the direction already established by the two points of the tree and the peg, for the distance of fifty feet—Jupiter clearing away the brambles with the scythe. At the spot thus attained a second peg was driven, and about this, as a center, a rude circle, about four feet in diameter, described. Taking now a spade himself, and giving one to Jupiter and one to me, Legrand begged us to set about digging as quickly as possible.

To speak the truth, I had no especial relish for such amusement at any time, and, at that particular moment, would willingly have declined it; for the night was coming on, and I felt much fatigued with the exercise already taken; but I saw no mode of escape, and was fearful of disturbing my poor friend's equanimity by a refusal. Could I have depended, indeed, upon Jupiter's aid, I would have had no hesitation in attempting to get the lunatic home by force; but I was too well assured of the old negro's disposition, to hope that he would assist me, under any circumstances, in a personal contest with his master. I made no doubt that the latter had been infected with some of the innumerable Southern superstitions about money buried, and that his fantasy had received confirmation by the finding of the scarabaeus, or, perhaps, by Jupiter's obstinacy in maintaining it to be "a bug of real gold." A mind disposed to lunacy would readily be led away by such suggestions—especially if chiming in with favorite preconceived ideas—and then I called to mind the poor fellow's speech about the beetle's being "the index of his fortune." Upon the whole, I was sadly vexed and puzzled, but, at length, I concluded to make a virtue of necessity—to dig with a good will, and thus the sooner to convince the visionary, by ocular demonstration, of the fallacy of the opinion he entertained.

The lanterns having been lit, we all fell to work with a zeal worthy a more rational cause; and, as the glare fell upon our persons and implements, I could not help thinking how picturesque a group we composed, and how strange and suspicious our labors must have appeared to any interloper who, by chance, might have stumbled upon our whereabouts.

We dug very steadily for two hours. Little was said; and our chief embarrassment lay in the yelpings of the dog, who took exceeding interest in our proceedings. He, at length, became so obstreperous that we grew fearful of his giving the alarm to some stragglers in the vicinity,—or, rather, this was the apprehension of Legrand;— for myself, I should have rejoiced at any interruption which might have enabled me to get the wanderer home. The noise was, at length, very effectually silenced by Jupiter, who, getting out of the hole with a dogged air of deliberation, tied the brute's mouth up with one of his suspenders, and then returned, with a grave chuckle, to his task.

When the time mentioned had expired, we had reached a depth of five feet, and yet no signs of any treasure became manifest. A general pause ensued, and I began to hope that the farce was at an end. Legrand, however, although evidently much disconcerted, wiped his brow thoughtfully and recommenced. We had excavated the entire circle of four feet diameter, and now we slightly enlarged the limit, and went to the farther depth of two feet. Still nothing appeared. The gold-seeker, whom I sincerely pitied, at length clambered from the pit, with the bitterest disappointment imprinted upon every feature, and proceeded, slowly and reluctantly, to put on his coat, which he had thrown off at the beginning of his labor. In the meantime I made no remark. Jupiter, at a signal from his master, began to gather up his tools. This done, and the dog having been unmuzzled, we turned in profound silence toward home.

We had taken, perhaps, a dozen steps in this direction, when, with a loud oath, Legrand strode up to Jupiter, and seized him by the collar. The astonished negro opened his eyes and mouth to the fullest extent, let fall the spades, and fell upon his knees.

"You scoundrel!" said Legrand, hissing out the syllables from between his clenched teeth—"you infernal black villain!—speak, I tell you!—answer me this instant, without prevarication!—which— which is your left eye?"

"Oh, my golly, Massa Will! aint dis here my lef eye for sartain?" roared the terrified Jupiter, placing his hand upon his RIGHT organ of vision, and holding it there with a desperate pertinacity, as if in immediate, dread of his master's attempt at a gouge.

"I thought so!—I knew it! hurrah!" vociferated Legrand, letting the negro go and executing a series of curvets and caracols, much to the astonishment of his valet, who, arising from his knees, looked, mutely, from his master to myself, and then from myself to his master.

"Come! we must go back," said the latter, "the game's not up yet;" and he again led the way to the tulip tree.

"Jupiter," said he, when we reached its foot, "come here! was the skull nailed to the limb with the face outward, or with the face to the limb?"

"De face was out, massa, so dat de crows could get at de eyes good, widout any trouble."

"Well, then, was it this eye or that through which you dropped the beetle?" here Legrand touched each of Jupiter's eyes.

"'Twas dis eye, massa—de lef eye—jis as you tell me," and here it was his right eye that the negro indicated.

"That will do—we must try it again."

Here my friend, about whose madness I now saw, or fancied that I saw, certain indications of method, removed the peg which marked the spot where the beetle fell, to a spot about three inches to the westward of its former position. Taking, now, the tape measure from the nearest point of the trunk to the peg, as before, and continuing the extension in a straight line to the distance of fifty feet, a spot was indicated, removed, by several yards, from the point at which we had been digging.

Around the new position a circle, somewhat larger than in the former instance, was now described, and we again set to work with the spade. I was dreadfully weary, but, scarcely understanding what had occasioned the change in my thoughts, I felt no longer any great aversion from the labor imposed. I had become most unaccountably interested—nay, even excited. Perhaps there was something, amid all the extravagant demeanor of Legrand—some air of forethought, or of deliberation, which impressed me. I dug eagerly, and now and then caught myself actually looking, with something that very much resembled expectation, for the fancied treasure, the vision of which had demented my unfortunate companion. At a period when such vagaries of thought most fully possessed me, and when we had been at work perhaps an hour and a half, we were again interrupted by the violent howlings of the dog. His uneasiness, in the first instance, had been, evidently, but the result of playfulness or caprice, but he now assumed a bitter and serious tone. Upon Jupiter's again attempting to muzzle him, he made furious resistance, and, leaping into the hole, tore up the mold frantically with his claws. In a few seconds he had uncovered a mass of human bones, forming two complete skeletons, intermingled with several buttons of metal, and what appeared to be the dust of decayed woolen. One or two strokes of a spade upturned the blade of a large Spanish knife, and, as we dug farther, three or four loose pieces of gold and silver coin came to light.

At sight of these the joy of Jupiter could scarcely be restrained, but the countenance of his master wore an air of extreme disappointment. He urged us, however, to continue our exertions, and the words were hardly uttered when I stumbled and fell forward, having caught the toe of my boot in a large ring of iron that lay half buried in the loose earth.

We now worked in earnest, and never did I pass ten minutes of more intense excitement. During this interval we had fairly unearthed an oblong chest of wood, which, from its perfect preservation and wonderful hardness, had plainly been subjected to some mineralizing process—perhaps that of the bichloride of mercury. This box was three feet and a half long, three feet broad, and two and a half feet deep. It was firmly secured by bands of wrought iron, riveted, and forming a kind of open trelliswork over the whole. On each side of the chest, near the top, were three rings of iron—six in all—by means of which a firm hold could be obtained by six persons. Our utmost united endeavors served only to disturb the coffer very slightly in its bed. We at once saw the impossibility of removing so great a weight. Luckily, the sole fastenings of the lid consisted of two sliding bolts. These we drew back—trembling and panting with anxiety. In an instant, a treasure of incalculable value lay gleaming before us. As the rays of the lanterns fell within the pit, there flashed upward a glow and a glare, from a confused heap of gold and of jewels, that absolutely dazzled our eyes.

I shall not pretend to describe the feelings with which I gazed. Amazement was, of course, predominant. Legrand appeared exhausted with excitement, and spoke very few words. Jupiter's countenance wore, for some minutes, as deadly a pallor as it is possible, in the nature of things, for any negro's visage to assume. He seemed stupefied—thunderstricken. Presently he fell upon his knees in the pit, and burying his naked arms up to the elbows in gold, let them there remain, as if enjoying the luxury of a bath. At length, with a deep sigh, he exclaimed, as if in a soliloquy:

"And dis all cum of de goole-bug! de putty goole-bug! de poor little goole-bug, what I boosed in that sabage kind oh style! Ain't you shamed oh yourself, nigger?—answer me dat!"

It became necessary, at last, that I should arouse both master and valet to the expediency of removing the treasure. It was growing late, and it behooved us to make exertion, that we might get everything housed before daylight. It was difficult to say what should he done, and much time was spent in deliberation—so confused were the ideas of all. We, finally, lightened the box by removing two thirds of its contents, when we were enabled, with some trouble, to raise it from the hole. The articles taken out were deposited among the brambles, and the dog left to guard them, with strict orders from Jupiter neither, upon any pretense, to stir from the spot, nor to open his mouth until our return. We then hurriedly made for home with the chest; reaching the hut in safety, but after excessive toil, at one o'clock in the morning. Worn out as we were, it was not in human nature to do more immediately. We rested until two, and had supper; starting for the hills immediately afterwards, armed with three stout sacks, which, by good luck, were upon the premises. A little before four we arrived at the pit, divided the remainder of the booty, as equally as might be, among us, and, leaving the holes unfilled, again set out for the hut, at which, for the second time, we deposited our golden burdens, just as the first faint streaks of the dawn gleamed from over the treetops in the east.

We were now thoroughly broken down; but the intense excitement of the time denied us repose. After an unquiet slumber of some three or four hours' duration, we arose, as if by preconcert, to make examination of our treasure.

The chest had been full to the brim, and we spent the whole day, and the greater part of the next night, in a scrutiny of its contents. There had been nothing like order or arrangement. Everything had been heaped in promiscuously. Having assorted all with care, we found ourselves possessed of even vaster wealth than we had at first supposed. In coin there was rather more than four hundred and fifty thousand dollars—estimating the value of the pieces, as accurately as we could, by the tables of the period. There was not a particle of silver. All was gold of antique date and of great variety—French, Spanish, and German money, with a few English guineas, and some counters, of which we had never seen specimens before. There were several very large and heavy coins, so worn that we could make nothing of their inscriptions. There was no American money. The value of the jewels we found more difficulty in estimating. There were diamonds—some of them exceedingly large and fine—a hundred and ten in all, and not one of them small; eighteen rubies of remarkable brilliancy;—three hundred and ten emeralds, all very beautiful; and twenty-one sapphires, with an opal. These stones had all been broken from their settings and thrown loose in the chest. The settings themselves, which we picked out from among the other gold, appeared to have been beaten up with hammers, as if to prevent identification. Besides all this, there was a vast quantity of solid gold ornaments; nearly two hundred massive finger and ears rings; rich chains—thirty of these, if I remember; eighty-three very large and heavy crucifixes; five gold censers of great value; a prodigious golden punch bowl, ornamented with richly chased vine leaves and Bacchanalian figures; with two sword handles exquisitely embossed, and many other smaller articles which I cannot recollect. The weight of these valuables exceeded three hundred and fifty pounds avoirdupois; and in this estimate I have not included one hundred and ninety-seven superb gold watches; three of the number being worth each five hundred dollars, if one. Many of them were very old, and as timekeepers valueless; the works having suffered, more or less, from corrosion—but all were richly jeweled and in cases of great worth. We estimated the entire contents of the chest, that night, at a million and a half of dollars; and upon the subsequent disposal of the trinkets and jewels a few being retained for our own use, it was found that we had greatly undervalued the treasure.

When, at length, we had concluded our examination, and the intense excitement of the time had, in some measure, subsided, Legrand, who saw that I was dying with impatience for a solution of this most extraordinary riddle, entered into a full detail of all the circumstances connected with it.

"You remember," said he, "the night when I handed you the rough sketch I had made of the scarabaeus. You recollect, also, that I became quite vexed at you for insisting that my drawing resembled a death's head. When you first made this assertion I thought you were jesting; but afterwards I called to mind the peculiar spots on the back of the insect, and admitted to myself that your remark had some little foundation in fact. Still, the sneer at my graphic powers irritated me—for I am considered a good artist—and, therefore, when you handed me the scrap of parchment, I was about to crumple it up and throw it angrily into the fire."

"The scrap of paper, you mean," said I.

"No; it had much of the appearance of paper, and at first I supposed it to be such, but when I came to draw upon it, I discovered it at once to be a piece of very thin parchment. It was quite dirty, you remember. Well, as I was in the very act of crumpling it up, my glance fell upon the sketch at which you had been looking, and you may imagine my astonishment when I perceived, in fact, the figure of a death's head just where, it seemed to me, I had made the drawing of the beetle. For a moment I was too much amazed to think with accuracy. I knew that my design was very different in detail from this—although there was a certain similarity in general outline. Presently I took a candle, and seating myself at the other end of the room, proceeded to scrutinize the parchment more closely. Upon turning it over, I saw my own sketch upon the reverse, just as I had made it. My first idea, now, was mere surprise at the really remarkable similarity of outline—at the singular coincidence involved in the fact that, unknown to me, there should have been a skull upon the other side of the parchment, immediately beneath my figure of the scarabaeus, and that this skull, not only in outline, but in size, should so closely resemble my drawing. I say the singularity of this coincidence absolutely stupefied me for a time. This is the usual effect of such coincidences. The mind struggles to establish a connection—a sequence of cause and effect—and, being unable to do so, suffers a species of temporary paralysis. But, when I recovered from this stupor, there dawned upon me gradually a conviction which startled me even far more than the coincidence. I began distinctly, positively, to remember that there had been NO drawing upon the parchment, when I made my sketch of the scarabaeus. I became perfectly certain of this; for I recollected turning up first one side and then the other, in search of the cleanest spot. Had the skull been then there, of course I could not have failed to notice it. Here was indeed a mystery which I felt it impossible to explain; but, even at that early moment, there seemed to glimmer, faintly, within the most remote and secret chambers of my intellect, a glow-wormlike conception of that truth which last night's adventure brought to so magnificent a demonstration. I arose at once, and putting the parchment securely away, dismissed all further reflection until I should be alone.

"When you had gone, and when Jupiter was fast asleep, I betook myself to a more methodical investigation of the affair. In the first place I considered the manner in which the parchment had come into my possession. The spot where we discovered the scarabaeus was on the coast of the mainland, about a mile eastward of the island, and but a short distance above high-water mark. Upon my taking hold of it, it gave me a sharp bite, which caused me to let it drop. Jupiter, with his accustomed caution, before seizing the insect, which had flown toward him, looked about him for a leaf, or something of that nature, by which to take hold of it. It was at this moment that his eyes, and mine also, fell upon the scrap of parchment, which I then supposed to be paper. It was lying half buried in the sand, a corner sticking up. Near the spot where we found it, I observed the remnants of the hull of what appeared to have been a ship's longboat. The wreck seemed to have been there for a very great while, for the resemblance to boat timbers could scarcely be traced.

"Well, Jupiter picked up the parchment, wrapped the beetle in it, and gave it to me. Soon afterwards we turned to go home, and on the way met Lieutenant G——. I showed him the insect, and he begged me to let him take it to the fort. Upon my consenting, he thrust it forthwith into his waistcoat pocket, without the parchment in which it had been wrapped, and which I had continued to hold in my hand during his inspection. Perhaps he dreaded my changing my mind, and thought it best to make sure of the prize at once—you know how enthusiastic he is on all subjects connected with Natural History. At the same time, without being conscious of it, I must have deposited the parchment in my own pocket.

"You remember that when I went to the table, for the purpose of making a sketch of the beetle, I found no paper where it was usually kept. I looked in the drawer, and found none there. I searched my pockets, hoping to find an old letter, when my hand fell upon the parchment. I thus detail the precise mode in which it came into my possession, for the circumstances impressed me with peculiar force.

"No doubt you will think me fanciful—but I had already established a kind of CONNECTION. I had put together two links of a great chain. There was a boat lying upon a seacoast, and not far from the boat was a parchment—NOT A PAPER—with a skull depicted upon it. You will, of course, ask 'where is the connection?' I reply that the skull, or death's head, is the well-known emblem of the pirate. The flag of the death's head is hoisted in all engagements.

"I have said that the scrap was parchment, and not paper. Parchment is durable—almost imperishable. Matters of little moment are rarely consigned to parchment; since, for the mere ordinary purposes of drawing or writing, it is not nearly so well adapted as paper. This reflection suggested some meaning—some relevancy—in the death's head. I did not fail to observe, also, the FORM of the parchment. Although one of its corners had been, by some accident, destroyed, it could be seen that the original form was oblong. It was just such a slip, indeed, as might have been chosen for a memorandum—for a record of something to be long remembered, and carefully preserved."

"But," I interposed, "you say that the skull was NOT upon the parchment when you made the drawing of the beetle. How then do you trace any connection between the boat and the skull—since this latter, according to your own admission, must have been designed God only knows how or by whom at some period subsequent to your sketching the scarabaeus?"

"Ah, hereupon turns the whole mystery; although the secret, at this point, I had comparatively little difficulty in solving. My steps were sure, and could afford but a single result. I reasoned, for example, thus: When I drew the scarabaeus, there was no skull apparent upon the parchment. When I had completed the drawing I gave it to you, and observed you narrowly until you returned it. YOU, therefore, did not design the skull, and no one else was present to do it. Then it was not done by human agency. And nevertheless it was done.

"At this stage of my reflections I endeavored to remember, and DID remember, with entire distinctness, every incident which occurred about the period in question. The weather was chilly oh, rare and happy accident!, and a fire was blazing upon the hearth. I was heated with exercise and sat near the table. You, however, had drawn a chair close to the chimney. Just as I placed the parchment in your hand, and as you were in the act of inspecting it, Wolf, the Newfoundland, entered, and leaped upon your shoulders. With your left hand you caressed him and kept him off, while your right, holding the parchment, was permitted to fall listlessly between your knees, and in close proximity to the fire. At one moment I thought the blaze had caught it, and was about to caution you, but, before I could speak, you had withdrawn it, and were engaged in its examination. When I considered all these particulars, I doubted not for a moment that HEAT had been the agent in bringing to light, upon the parchment, the skull which I saw designed upon it. You are well aware that chemical preparations exist, and have existed time out of mind, by means of which it is possible to write upon either paper or vellum, so that the characters shall become visible only when subjected to the action of fire. Zaffre, digested in aqua regia, and diluted with four times its weight of water, is sometimes employed; a green tint results. The regulus of cobalt, dissolved in spirit of niter, gives a red. These colors disappear at longer or shorter intervals after the material written upon cools, but again become apparent upon the reapplication of heat.

"I now scrutinized the death's head with care. Its outer edges— the edges of the drawing nearest the edge of the vellum—were far more DISTINCT than the others. It was clear that the action of the caloric had been imperfect or unequal. I immediately kindled a fire, and subjected every portion of the parchment to a glowing heat. At first, the only effect was the strengthening of the faint lines in the skull; but, upon persevering in the experiment, there became visible, at the corner of the slip, diagonally opposite to the spot in which the death's head was delineated, the figure of what I at first supposed to be a goat. A closer scrutiny, however, satisfied me that it was intended for a kid."

"Ha! ha!" said I, "to be sure I have no right to laugh at you—a million and a half of money is too serious a matter for mirth—but you are not about to establish a third link in your chain—you will not find any especial connection between your pirates and a goat— pirates, you know, have nothing to do with goats; they appertain to the farming interest."

"But I have just said that the figure was NOT that of a goat."

"Well, a kid then—pretty much the same thing."

"Pretty much, but not altogether," said Legrand. "You may have heard of one CAPTAIN Kidd. I at once looked upon the figure of the animal as a kind of punning or hieroglyphical signature. I say signature; because its position upon the vellum suggested this idea. The death's head at the corner diagonally opposite, had, in the same manner, the air of a stamp, or seal. But I was sorely put out by the absence of all else—of the body to my imagined instrument—of the text for my context."

"I presume you expected to find a letter between the stamp and the signature."

"Something of that kind. The fact is, I felt irresistibly impressed with a presentiment of some vast good fortune impending. I can scarcely say why. Perhaps, after all, it was rather a desire than an actual belief;—but do you know that Jupiter's silly words, about the bug being of solid gold, had a remarkable effect upon my fancy? And then the series of accidents and coincidents—these were so VERY extraordinary. Do you observe how mere an accident it was that these events should have occurred upon the SOLE day of all the year in which it has been, or may be sufficiently cool for fire, and that without the fire, or without the intervention of the dog at the precise moment in which he appeared, I should never have become aware of the death's head, and so never the possessor of the treasure?"

"But proceed—I am all impatience."

"Well; you have heard, of course, the many stories current—the thousand vague rumors afloat about money buried, somewhere upon the Atlantic coast, by Kidd and his associates. These rumors must have had some foundation in fact. And that the rumors have existed so long and so continuous, could have resulted, it appeared to me, only from the circumstance of the buried treasures still REMAINING entombed. Had Kidd concealed his plunder for a time, and afterwards reclaimed it, the rumors would scarcely have reached us in their present unvarying form. You will observe that the stories told are all about money-seekers, not about money-finders. Had the pirate recovered his money, there the affair would have dropped. It seemed to me that some accident—say the loss of a memorandum indicating its locality—had deprived him of the means of recovering it, and that this accident had become known to his followers, who otherwise might never have heard that the treasure had been concealed at all, and who, busying themselves in vain, because unguided, attempts to regain it, had given first birth, and then universal currency, to the reports which are now so common. Have you ever heard of any important treasure being unearthed along the coast?"

"Never."

"But that Kidd's accumulations were immense, is well known. I took it for granted, therefore, that the earth still held them; and you will scarcely be surprised when I tell you that I felt a hope, nearly amounting to certainty, that the parchment so strangely found involved a lost record of the place of deposit."

"But how did you proceed?"

"I held the vellum again to the fire, after increasing the heat, but nothing appeared. I now thought it possible that the coating of dirt might have something to do with the failure: so I carefully rinsed the parchment by pouring warm water over it, and, having done this, I placed it in a tin pan, with the skull downward, and put the pan upon a furnace of lighted charcoal. In a few minutes, the pan having become thoroughly heated, I removed the slip, and, to my inexpressible joy, found it spotted, in several places, with what appeared to be figures arranged in lines. Again I placed it in the pan, and suffered it to remain another minute. Upon taking it off, the whole was just as you see it now."

Here Legrand, having reheated the parchment, submitted it to my inspection. The following characters were rudely traced, in a red tint, between the death's head and the goat:

"53++!3056*;48264+4+.;806*;48!8]6085;1+8*:+;:

+*8!83885*!;

46;88*96*?;8*+;485;5*!2:*+;4956*25*-48]8*;4069285;6!

84++;

1+9;48081;8:8+1;48!85;4485!528806*81+9;48;88;4+?34 ;484+;161;: 188;+?;" "But," said I, returning him the slip, "I am as much in the dark as ever. Were all the jewels of Golconda awaiting me upon my solution of this enigma, I am quite sure that I should be unable to earn them."

"And yet," said Legrand, "the solution is by no means so difficult as you might be led to imagine from the first hasty inspection of the characters. These characters, as anyone might readily guess, form a cipher—that is to say, they convey a meaning; but then from what is known of Kidd, I could not suppose him capable of constructing any of the more abstruse cryptographs. I made up my mind, at once, that this was of a simple species—such, however, as would appear, to the crude intellect of the sailor, absolutely insoluble without the key."

"And you really solved it?"

"Readily; I have solved others of an abstruseness ten thousand times greater. Circumstances, and a certain bias of mind, have led me to take interest in such riddles, and it may well be doubted whether human ingenuity can construct an enigma of the kind which human ingenuity may not, by proper application, resolve. In fact, having once established connected and legible characters, I scarcely gave a thought to the mere difficulty of developing their import.

"In the present case—indeed in all cases of secret writing—the first question regards the LANGUAGE of the cipher; for the principles of solution, so far, especially, as the more simple ciphers are concerned, depend upon, and are varied by, the genius of the particular idiom. In general, there is no alternative but experiment directed by probabilities of every tongue known to him who attempts the solution, until the true one be attained. But, with the cipher now before us, all difficulty was removed by the signature. The pun upon the word 'Kidd' is appreciable in no other language than the English. But for this consideration I should have begun my attempts with the Spanish and French, as the tongues in which a secret of this kind would most naturally have been written by a pirate of the Spanish main. As it was, I assumed the cryptograph to be English.

"You observe there are no divisions between the words. Had there been divisions the task would have been comparatively easy. In such cases I should have commenced with a collation and analysis of the shorter words, and, had a word of a single letter occurred, as is most likely, a or I, for example, I should have considered the solution as assured. But, there being no division, my first step was to ascertain the predominant letters, as well as the least frequent. Counting all, I constructed a table thus:

Of the character 8 there are 33.

; " 26.

4 " 19.

+ " 16.

* " 13.

5 " 12.

6 " 11.

!1 " 8.

0 " 6.

92 " 5.

:3 " 4.

? " 3.

] " 2.

-. " 1.

"Now, in English, the letter which most frequently occurs is e. Afterwards, the succession runs thus: a o i d h n r s t u y c f g l m w b k p q x z. E predominates so remarkably, that an individual sentence of any length is rarely seen, in which it is not the prevailing character.

"Here, then, we have, in the very beginning, the groundwork for something more than a mere guess. The general use which may be made of the table is obvious—but, in this particular cipher, we shall only very partially require its aid. As our predominant character is 8, we will commence by assuming it as the e of the natural alphabet. To verify the supposition, let us observe if the 8 be seen often in couples—for e is doubled with great frequency in English—in such words, for example, as 'meet,' 'fleet,' 'speed,' 'seen,' 'been,' 'agree,' etc. In the present instance we see it doubled no less than five times, although the cryptograph is brief.

"Let us assume 8, then, as e. Now, of all WORDS in the language, 'the' is most usual; let us see, therefore, whether there are not repetitions of any three characters, in the same order of collocation, the last of them being 8. If we discover repetitions of such letters, so arranged, they will most probably represent the word 'the.' Upon inspection, we find no less than seven such arrangements, the characters being ;48. We may, therefore, assume that ; represents t, 4 represents h, and 8 represents e—the last being now well confirmed. Thus a great step has been taken.

"But, having established a single word, we are enabled to establish a vastly important point; that is to say, several commencements and terminations of other words. Let us refer, for example, to the last instance but one, in which the combination ;48 occurs—not far from the end of the cipher. We know that the ; immediately ensuing is the commencement of a word, and, of the six characters succeeding this 'the,' we are cognizant of no less than five. Let us set these characters down, thus, by the letters we know them to represent, leaving a space for the unknown—

t eeth.

"Here we are enabled, at once, to discard the 'th,' as forming no portion of the word commencing with the first t; since, by experiment of the entire alphabet for a letter adapted to the vacancy, we perceive that no word can be formed of which this th can be a part. We are thus narrowed into

t ee,

and, going through the alphabet, if necessary, as before, we arrive at the word 'tree,' as the sole possible reading. We thus gain another letter, r, represented by , with the words 'the tree' in juxtaposition.

"Looking beyond these words, for a short distance, we again see the combination ;48, and employ it by way of TERMINATION to what immediately precedes. We have thus this arrangement:

the tree ;44+?34 the,

or, substituting the natural letters, where known, it reads thus:

the tree thr+?3h the.

"Now, if, in place of the unknown characters, we leave blank spaces, or substitute dots, we read thus:

the tree thr… h the,

when the word 'through' makes itself evident at once. But this discovery gives us three new letters, o, u, and g, represented by +, ?, and 3.

"Looking now, narrowly, through the cipher for combinations of known characters, we find, not very far from the beginning, this arrangement,

8388, or egree,

which plainly, is the conclusion of the word 'degree,' and gives us another letter, d, represented by !.

"Four letters beyond the word 'degree,' we perceive the combination

;46;88.

"Translating the known characters, and representing the unknown by dots, as before, we read thus:

th.rtee,

an arrangement immediately suggestive of the word thirteen,' and again furnishing us with two new characters, i and n, represented by 6 and *.

"Referring, now, to the beginning of the cryptograph, we find the combination,

53++!.

"Translating as before, we obtain

.good,

which assures us that the first letter is A, and that the first two words are 'A good.'

"It is now time that we arrange our key, as far as discovered, in a tabular form, to avoid confusion. It will stand thus:

5 represents a

! " d

8 " e

3 " g

4 " h

6 " i

* " n

+ " o

" r

; " t

? " u

"We have, therefore, no less than eleven of the most important letters represented, and it will be unnecessary to proceed with the details of the solution. I have said enough to convince you that ciphers of this nature are readily soluble, and to give you some insight into the rationale of their development. But be assured that the specimen before us appertains to the very simplest species of cryptograph. It now only remains to give you the full translation of the characters upon the parchment, as unriddled. Here it is:

"'A good glass in the bishop's hostel in the devil's seat forty-one degrees and thirteen minutes northeast and by north main branch seventh limb east side shoot from the left eye of the death's head a bee-line from the tree through the shot fifty feet out.'"

"But," said I, "the enigma seems still in as bad a condition as ever. How is it possible to extort a meaning from all this jargon about 'devil's seats,' 'death's heads,' and 'bishop's hostels'?"

"I confess," replied Legrand, "that the matter still wears a serious aspect, when regarded with a casual glance. My first endeavor was to divide the sentence into the natural division intended by the cryptographist."

"You mean, to punctuate it?"

"Something of that kind."

"But how was it possible to effect this?"

"I reflected that it had been a POINT with the writer to run his words together without division, so as to increase the difficulty of solution. Now, a not overacute man, in pursuing such an object, would be nearly certain to overdo the matter. When, in the course of his composition, he arrived at a break in his subject which would naturally require a pause, or a point, he would be exceedingly apt to run his characters, at this place, more than usually close together. If you will observe the MS., in the present instance, you will easily detect five such cases of unusual crowding. Acting upon this hint I made the division thus:

"'A good glass in the bishop's hostel in the devil's seat—forty- one degrees and thirteen minutes—northeast and by north—main branch seventh limb east side—shoot from the left eye of the death's head—a bee-line from the tree through the shot fifty feet out.'"

"Even this division," said I, "leaves me still in the dark."

"It left me also in the dark," replied Legrand, "for a few days; during which I made diligent inquiry in the neighborhood of Sullivan's Island, for any building which went by name of the 'Bishop's Hotel'; for, of course, I dropped the obsolete word 'hostel.' Gaining no information on the subject, I was on the point of extending my sphere of search, and proceeding in a more systematic manner, when, one morning, it entered into my head, quite suddenly, that this 'Bishop's Hostel' might have some reference to an old family, of the name of Bessop, which, time out of mind, had held possession of an ancient manor house, about four miles to the northward of the island. I accordingly went over to the plantation, and reinstituted my inquiries among the older negroes of the place. At length one of the most aged of the women said that she had heard of such a place as Bessop's Castle, and thought that she could guide me to it, but that it was not a castle, nor a tavern, but a high rock.

"I offered to pay her well for her trouble, and, after some demur, she consented to accompany me to the spot. We found it without much difficulty, when, dismissing her, I proceeded to examine the place. The 'castle' consisted of an irregular assemblage of cliffs and rocks—one of the latter being quite remarkable for its height as well as for its insulated and artificial appearance. I clambered to its apex, and then felt much at a loss as to what should be next done.

"While I was busied in reflection, my eyes fell upon a narrow ledge in the eastern face of the rock, perhaps a yard below the summit upon which I stood. This ledge projected about eighteen inches, and was not more than a foot wide, while a niche in the cliff just above it gave it a rude resemblance to one of the hollow-backed chairs used by our ancestors. I made no doubt that here was the 'devil's seat' alluded to in the MS., and now I seemed to grasp the full secret of the riddle.

"The 'good glass,' I knew, could have reference to nothing but a telescope; for the word 'glass' is rarely employed in any other sense by seamen. Now here, I at once saw, was a telescope to be used, and a definite point of view, ADMITTING NO VARIATION, from which to use it. Nor did I hesitate to believe that the phrases, 'forty-one degrees and thirteen minutes,' and 'northeast and by north,' were intended as directions for the leveling of the glass. Greatly excited by these discoveries, I hurried home, procured a telescope, and returned to the rock.

"I let myself down to the ledge, and found that it was impossible to retain a seat upon it except in one particular position. This fact confirmed my preconceived idea. I proceeded to use the glass. Of course, the 'forty-one degrees and thirteen minutes' could allude to nothing but elevation above the visible horizon, since the horizontal direction was clearly indicated by the words, 'northeast and by north.' This latter direction I at once established by means of a pocket compass; then, pointing the glass as nearly at an angle of forty-one degrees of elevation as I could do it by guess, I moved it cautiously up or down, until my attention was arrested by a circular rift or opening in the foliage of a large tree that overtopped its fellows in the distance. In the center of this rift I perceived a white spot, but could not, at first, distinguish what it was. Adjusting the focus of the telescope, I again looked, and now made it out to be a human skull.

"Upon this discovery I was so sanguine as to consider the enigma solved; for the phrase 'main branch, seventh limb, east side,' could refer only to the position of the skull upon the tree, while 'shoot from the left eye of the death's head' admitted, also, of but one interpretation, in regard to a search for buried treasure. I perceived that the design was to drop a bullet from the left eye of the skull, and that a bee-line, or, in other words, a straight line, drawn from the nearest point of the trunk 'through the shot' or the spot where the bullet fell, and thence extended to a distance of fifty feet, would indicate a definite point—and beneath this point I thought it at least POSSIBLE that a deposit of value lay concealed."

"All this," I said, "is exceedingly clear, and, although ingenious, still simple and explicit. When you left the Bishop's Hotel, what then?"

"Why, having carefully taken the bearings of the tree, I turned homeward. The instant that I left 'the devil's seat,' however, the circular rift vanished; nor could I get a glimpse of it afterwards, turn as I would. What seems to me the chief ingenuity in this whole business, is the fact for repeated experiment has convinced me it IS a fact that the circular opening in question is visible from no other attainable point of view than that afforded by the narrow ledge upon the face of the rock.

"In this expedition to the 'Bishop's Hotel' I had been attended by Jupiter, who had, no doubt, observed, for some weeks past, the abstraction of my demeanor, and took especial care not to leave me alone. But, on the next day, getting up very early, I contrived to give him the slip, and went into the hills in search of the tree. After much toil I found it. When I came home at night my valet proposed to give me a flogging. With the rest of the adventure I believe you are as well acquainted as myself."

"I suppose," said I, "you missed the spot, in the first attempt at digging, through Jupiter's stupidity in letting the bug fall through the right instead of through the left eye of the skull."

"Precisely. This mistake made a difference of about two inches and a half in the 'shot'—that is to say, in the position of the peg nearest the tree; and had the treasure been BENEATH the 'shot,' the error would have been of little moment; but 'the shot,' together with the nearest point of the tree, were merely two points for the establishment of a line of direction; of course the error, however trivial in the beginning, increased as we proceeded with the line, and by the time we had gone fifty feet threw us quite off the scent. But for my deep-seated impressions that treasure was here somewhere actually buried, we might have had all our labor in vain."

"But your grandiloquence, and your conduct in swinging the beetle— how excessively odd! I was sure you were mad. And why did you insist upon letting fall the bug, instead of a bullet, from the skull?"

"Why, to be frank, I felt somewhat annoyed by your evident suspicions touching my sanity, and so resolved to punish you quietly, in my own way, by a little bit of sober mystification. For this reason I swung the beetle, and for this reason I let it fall from the tree. An observation of yours about its great weight suggested the latter idea."

"Yes, I perceive; and now there is only one point which puzzles me. What are we to make of the skeletons found in the hole?"

"That is a question I am no more able to answer than yourself. There seems, however, only one plausible way of accounting for them—and yet it is dreadful to believe in such atrocity as my suggestion would imply. It is clear that Kidd—if Kidd indeed secreted this treasure, which I doubt not—it is clear that he must have had assistance in the labor. But this labor concluded, he may have thought it expedient to remove all participants in his secret. Perhaps a couple of blows with a mattock were sufficient, while his coadjutors were busy in the pit; perhaps it required a dozen—who shall tell?"

Made in the USA
Monee, IL
21 July 2020